Special thanks to K. F., H. McG., R. A., & P. J.

First edition 2010

Library of Congress Cataloging-in-Publication Data
Pien, Lark.
Mr. Elephanter / Lark Pien. — 1st ed.
p. cm.
Summary: From early morning until sunset, beloved Mr. Elephanter takes care of the
rambunctious youngsters of the Elephantery, preparing their breakfast, taking them
to the park, tucking them in for naps, and joining them at play.
ISBN 978-0-7636-4409-3
[1. Nannies — Fiction. 2. Elephants — Fiction.] I. Title.
PZ7.P587Mr 2010
[E] — dc22   2010007577

10 11 12 13 14 15 16 SCP 10 9 8 7 6 5 4 3 2 1

Printed in Humen, Dongguan, China

This book was typeset in Providence Sans.
The illustrations were done in watercolor.

Candlewick Press
99 Dover Street
Somerville, Massachusetts 02144

visit us at www.candlewick.com

Mr. Elephanter

Lark Pien

CANDLEWICK PRESS

Mr. Elephanter arrives early in the morning at the Elephantery. He's here to look after the young and peppy elephanties.

poom!

fwee!

fwee!

With tootles and trumpets, they greet Mr. Elephanter at the door. There are hugs and hellos all around.

Mr. Elephanter prepares banana pancakes for breakfast in the kitchen. The elephanties watch as he flips each one from pan to plate.

The little elephanties gobble their towering stack in no time flat.

Mr. Elephanter prefers to eat his pancakes one bite at a time.

When it is sunny outside, they go to swim in the neighborhood pool. The elephanties paddle and splash and show off their tricks.

When they are done, Mr. Elephanter rinses and dries them off.

But sometimes the elephanties want to air-dry instead!

fwee!

fwee!

From the pool, they parade together through the busy, bustling city. Mr. Elephanter watches for traffic, the shop owners wave, and the elephanties tootle at the cars zooming by.

They stop by the park to explore every nook and cranny. Mr. Elephanter spots an old friend just beyond a bank of trees.

The big elephant makes the leaves rustle with his rumbling chuckle. The elephanties run around his large knobby knees.

They chat for a long, long time before Mr. Elephanter and the tired elephanties head back to the Elephantery for some rest.

When they return, Mr. Elephanter tucks the elephanties into their beds for a nap. Then he takes a break, too.

It is enough time to catch up on small things.

Sometimes Mr. Elephanter hears a rumble and a tumble when the elephanties wake up . . .

and get into trouble!

It's more fun when everyone gets along.
Whether they're standing still as mountains . . .

or dancing all around.

At playtime, Mr. Elephanter pretends to be a tunnel, a tower, and a bridge. The elephanties crawl under, climb up, and march on top of him!

But when Mr. Elephanter gets a boo-boo,
the elephanties stop to take care of him too.

When the sun sets, it is time for Mr. Elephanter to leave the Elephantery. He puts on his coat, and the elephanties help with his hat.

There are hugs and good-byes all around.

The little elephanties wave good night as Mr. Elephanter heads for home under the starry sky.

See you
tomorrow!

31901050310392